THE AMAZ
SPIDER-MAN
SOUL OF THE HUNTER

J.M. DeMATTEIS MIKE ZECK BOB McLEOD

J.M. DeMATTEIS
Writer

MIKE ZECK
Penciler

BOB McLEOD
Inker

RICK PARKER
Letterer

STEVE BUCCELLATTO
Colorist

JOE KAUFMAN
Design

ERIC FEIN
Assistant Editor

DANNY FINGEROTH
Editor

TOM DeFALCO
Editor in Chief

HERE LIES
SERGEI
KRAVINOFF
KRAVEN THE HUNTER
HE DIED WITH
HONOR

PERFECT DAY FOR A FUNERAL.
...AND KEEP THE CHANGE--
HURRY UP, PETER-- I'M FREEZING.
ME, TOO. CHILLED TO THE BONE. BUT IT'S NOT THE WEATHER. IT'S THIS PLACE.
DOESN'T MATTER HOW ELEGANT THE BUILDING... HOW RITZY THE NEIGHBORHOOD. YOU CAN'T MAKE A FUNERAL HOME ANYTHING BUT UGLY. YOU CAN'T PUT A PRETTY MASK ON DEATH.

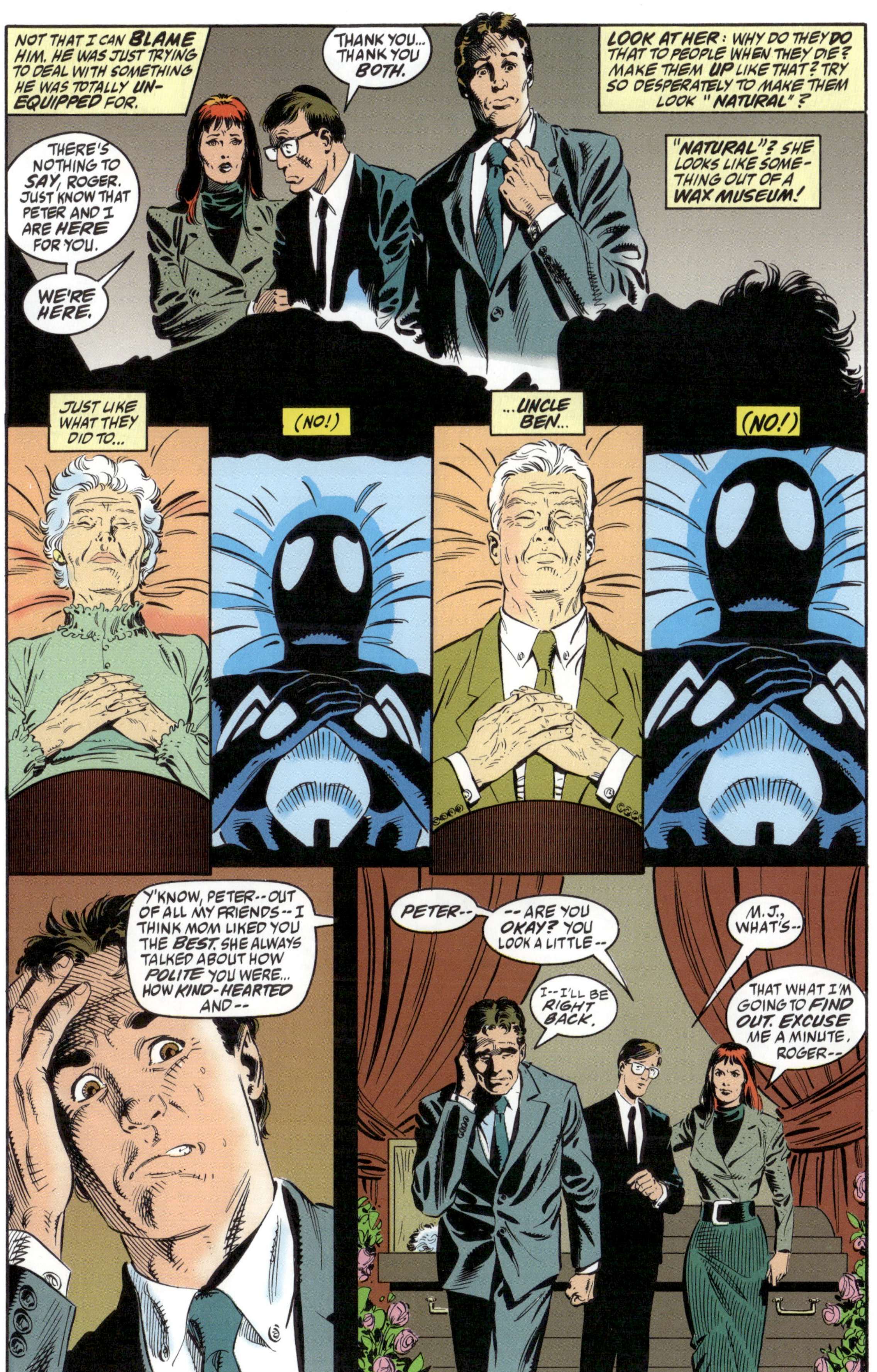
NOT THAT I CAN BLAME HIM. HE WAS JUST TRYING TO DEAL WITH SOMETHING HE WAS TOTALLY UN-EQUIPPED FOR.
THANK YOU... THANK YOU BOTH.
LOOK AT HER: WHY DO THEY DO THAT TO PEOPLE WHEN THEY DIE? MAKE THEM UP LIKE THAT? TRY SO DESPERATELY TO MAKE THEM LOOK "NATURAL"?
THERE'S NOTHING TO SAY, ROGER. JUST KNOW THAT PETER AND I ARE HERE FOR YOU.
WE'RE HERE.
"NATURAL"? SHE LOOKS LIKE SOME-THING OUT OF A WAX MUSEUM!
JUST LIKE WHAT THEY DID TO...
(NO!)
...UNCLE BEN...
(NO!)
Y'KNOW, PETER--OUT OF ALL MY FRIENDS--I THINK MOM LIKED YOU THE BEST. SHE ALWAYS TALKED ABOUT HOW POLITE YOU WERE... HOW KIND-HEARTED AND--
PETER--
--ARE YOU OKAY? YOU LOOK A LITTLE--
I--I'LL BE RIGHT BACK.
M.J., WHAT'S--
THAT WHAT I'M GOING TO FIND OUT. EXCUSE ME A MINUTE, ROGER--

SWEETIE...?
HUH?!
OH... M.J.-- YOU--
SWEETIE, WHAT IS IT? I'VE NEVER SEEN YOU SO JUMPY--

NOTHING. I-IT'S NOTHING.
OH, PLEASE-- YOU'RE WHITE AS A SHEET YOUR SUIT'S SOAKED IN SWEAT--
I KNOW YOU DON'T LIKE FUNERALS, SWEETIE, BUT--

IT'S NOTHING.
I SWEAR TO YOU, IT'S--

DON'T SWEAR ANYTHING. THERE'S SOMETHING WRONG--
MUST BE-- GETTING SICK OR SOMETHING. MAYBE THE FLU.
IT'S NOT JUST TODAY, PETER-- YOU'VE BEEN ACTING ODD FOR WEEKS NOW. YOU--

HERE LIES
SERGEI
KRAVINOFF
KRAVEN THE HUNTER
HE DIED WITH

JUST A LITTLE AIR.

GREAT, PARKER... JUST GREAT.
YOUR WIFE TRIES TO HELP YOU-- AND YOU BLOW HER OFF. YOUR FRIEND NEEDS YOU AND YOU RUN OUT ON HER.
BAD ENOUGH YOU HAVEN'T EVEN SEEN ROGER IN MONTHS. BUT TO ACT LIKE THIS WHEN HIS MOTHER'S JUST DIED--?
WHAT'S WRONG WITH ME?
NOTHING'S WRONG. NOTHING AT ALL. I PUT ON THE SPIDER SUIT... SWING OUT OVER THE CITY...

(IN THE GRAVE.)
...AND I'M JUST FINE.
(IN THE GROUND.)
FINE AND DANDY.
(TWO WEEKS!)

NO, DON'T THINK ABOUT IT! WHY THINK ABOUT IT? WHAT'S THE POINT? IT'S DONE, GONE, DEAD...
...AND BURIED...
HE BURIED ME! BURIED ME ALIVE! BUT NOT ALIVE! LESS THAN ALIVE! DEAD? NO!
(STOPIT STOPIT STOPIT!)
ALL THIS TIME, I'VE BEEN OKAY. BUT, LATELY... LATELY-- IT'S AS IF HE--
(STOPSTOPSTOP --JUSTSTOP THINKING ABOUT IT!!)
NO! THAT'S JUST CRAZY! UNLESS-- UNLESS I'M CRAZY! WHAT IF I'VE FINALLY--

DANGER? YES! SPIDER-SENSE PICKING UP DANGER!
GOOD. GIVE ME A CHANCE TO DO WHAT I DO BEST.

BE A HERO.
FORGET ALL THIS NONSENSE.
GONNA BE ALL RIGHT, PARKER.

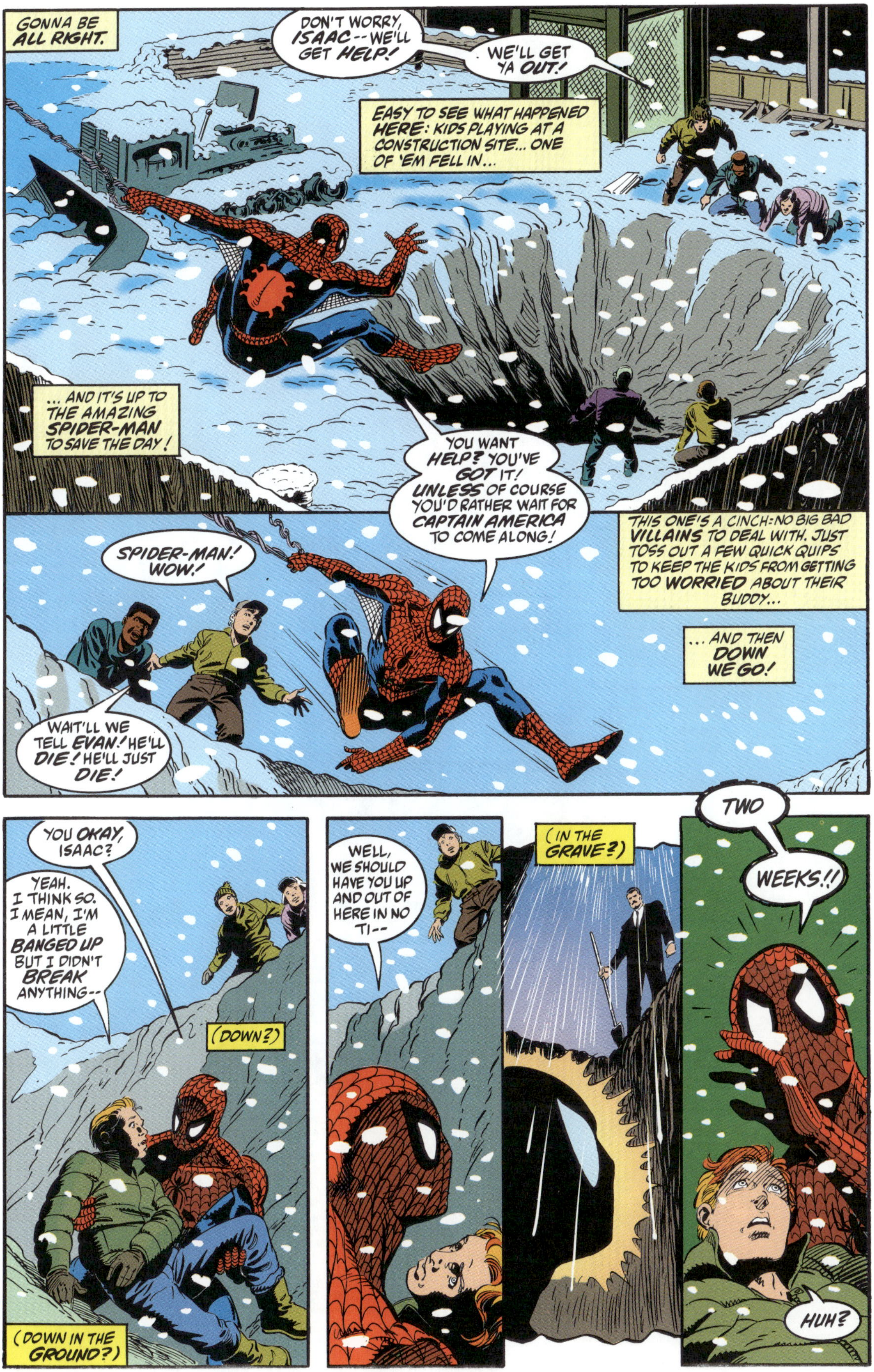

GONNA BE ALL RIGHT.
DON'T WORRY, ISAAC--WE'LL GET HELP!
WE'LL GET YA OUT!
EASY TO SEE WHAT HAPPENED HERE: KIDS PLAYING AT A CONSTRUCTION SITE... ONE OF 'EM FELL IN...
...AND IT'S UP TO THE AMAZING SPIDER-MAN TO SAVE THE DAY!
YOU WANT HELP? YOU'VE GOT IT! UNLESS OF COURSE YOU'D RATHER WAIT FOR CAPTAIN AMERICA TO COME ALONG!

THIS ONE'S A CINCH: NO BIG BAD VILLAINS TO DEAL WITH. JUST TOSS OUT A FEW QUICK QUIPS TO KEEP THE KIDS FROM GETTING TOO WORRIED ABOUT THEIR BUDDY...
SPIDER-MAN! WOW!
WAIT'LL WE TELL EVAN! HE'LL DIE! HE'LL JUST DIE!
...AND THEN DOWN WE GO!

TWO WEEKS, YOU MANIAC!!
YOU'RE NOT GONNA DO IT TO ME AGAIN!
WHAT'S HE TALKIN' ABOUT?
I DUNNO! MAYBE HE'S NUTS OR SOMETHIN'!

NOT CRAZY! I'M NOT!
HE DID IT TO ME! HE KILLED ME! HE BURIED ME! TWO WEEKS IN THE GRAVE... IN THE GROUND... DEAD!

HEY... SPIDER-MAN? WH- WHATSA MATTER?
DEAD!

GOTTA GET UP! OUT! FREE!

MARY JANE... HONEY... I LOVE YOU! DON'T LET ME DIE HERE AGAIN, MARY JANE! PLEASE--

DON'T
LET
HIM
KILL
ME
AGAIN!

NO MORE.

PLEASE, GOD...

THE HUNTER
DIED.

...IS THE CASTING OFF OF AN OLD COAT. NOT AN ENDING, BUT A PASSING OVER... A TRANSITION INTO A BETTER LIFE.

YET IF DEATH IS MERELY THE CASTING OFF OF AN OLD COAT, CAN WE BLAME OURSELVES FOR BEING ATTACHED TO THAT COAT?

ESTHER HOCHBERG'S SPIRIT MAY HAVE LEFT THIS WORLD... MAY HAVE FOUND A NEW LIFE WITH GOD... BUT WE REMAIN BEHIND--

SO THE PAIN FALLS TO US. AND WE DEAL WITH OUR PAIN BY FINDING JOY IN REMEMBERING.
HOW LUCKY WE ARE THAT SO MUCH IN ESTHER'S LIFE WAS WORTH REMEMBERING, WORTH REJOICING IN. MANY OF YOU WILL STAND UP HERE TODAY, SHARING THOSE JOYFUL MEMORIES. AND, YES, SHARING YOUR GRIEF AND PAIN.
BUT ONE THING I THINK WE MUST NOT SHARE TODAY--IS OUR FEAR. FEAR OF A FUTURE WITHOUT ESTHER. FEAR OF DEATH ITSELF. TOO MUCH OF OUR PRECIOUS LIFESPAN IS WASTED IN FEAR.

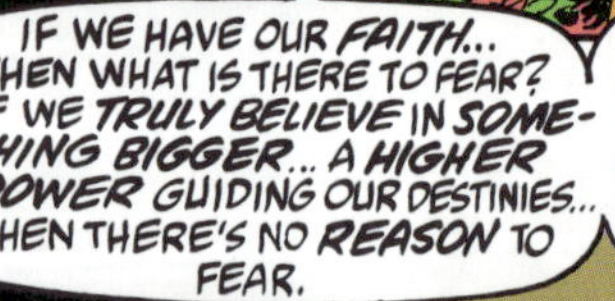
IF WE HAVE OUR FAITH... THEN WHAT IS THERE TO FEAR? IF WE TRULY BELIEVE IN SOMETHING BIGGER... A HIGHER POWER GUIDING OUR DESTINIES... THEN THERE'S NO REASON TO FEAR.

SO, TODAY, LET US MOURN ESTHER'S PASSING... LET US REJOICE IN THE MEMORIES SHE LEFT US--

--AND LET US HELP EACH OTHER--

--TO LET GO THE HAND OF FEAR--
...NO MORE.

...SO I SAID TO HIM, "THAT IS THE CRUMMIEST LINE OF DIALOGUE I'VE EVER HEARD--

"-- AND I REFUSE TO READ IT!"
AND HE TELLS ME, "I'M THE DIRECTOR, I THINK IT'S FINE-- AND YOU'RE GOING TO READ IT."
NOW I'M TALKING BIG, BUT INSIDE, I'M SHAKING LIKE A LEAF AND--
PETER? YOU LISTENING TO ME? THAT'S WHAT I THOUGHT. SIGH OKAY, LET'S TRY THIS AGAIN--

...SO I SAID TO HIM, "Y'KNOW, YOU'RE A PRETTY HANDSOME GUY. I THINK I'LL DUMP MY HUSBAND AND RUN AWAY WITH YOU."
NEXT THING I KNOW, THE BIG APE RIPS MY CLOTHES OFF, THROWS ME OVER HIS SHOULDER--
--AND CARRIES ME UP THE SIDE OF THE EMPIRE STATE BUILDING.

M.J.--
HA! I KNEW THAT'D GET YOU.
--DO YOU THINK IT'S TRUE?
WHAT? ABOUT ME AND THE APE?

WHAT THE RABBI SAID TODAY... ABOUT DEATH BEING LIKE THROWING AWAY AN OLD COAT.
OH, PETER--

DO YOU THINK IT'S TRUE?
Y'KNOW, WHEN I WAS A LITTLE GIRL, I WAS AT MY FRIEND SHERI'S HOUSE... AND SHERI'S FATHER-- RIGHT IN THE MIDDLE OF DINNER, HE GOT ALL WHITE--
-- THEN HE JUST KEELED OVER. HIT THE FLOOR.

IT WAS ALL SO QUICK-- SHERI'S BROTHERS CARRIED HIM INTO THE LIVING ROOM... HER MOM CALLED THE DOCTOR... BUT IT WAS TOO LATE.
AND ME? I DIDN'T KNOW WHAT WAS GOING ON. I WAS JUST STANDING THERE LIKE A JERK BY THE COUCH... AND, PETER-- I WATCHED HIM DIE!
THAT'S HORRIBLE.
NO... YES... BUT, THE POINT IS, I SWEAR TO YOU, I COULD SEE THE MOMENT OF DEATH. HE SUDDENLY WENT FROM BEING... I DUNNO... REAL-- -- TO BEING... WELL, ALL OF A SUDDEN HE LOOKED-- MORE LIKE AN AFTER-IMAGE THAN A MAN--
LIKE HIS FACE WAS JUST A MASK OF WHAT HE'D BEEN JUST A FEW SECONDS BEFORE. LIKE SOMETHING... SOME SPARK... THE ESSENCE OF WHAT HE WAS-- WAS JUST GONE.

HIS SOUL?
YES! HIS SOUL! HIS SOUL WAS GONE-- AND WHAT WAS LEFT BEHIND WAS JUST... AN OLD COAT.
BUT YOU CAN'T KNOW THAT. YOU CAN'T REALLY KNOW THAT.

MY MIND MAY DOUBT IT... BUT MY HEART...

...MY HEART'S NEVER DOUBTED IT FOR A SECOND.
I WANT TO BELIEVE THE WAY SHE DOES.

I'D GIVE ANYTHING TO BELIEVE!

AND WHEN SHE LOVES ME LIKE THIS-- WHEN WE SEEM TO BECOME... SOMETHING BIGGER--TOUCH SOMETHING HIGHER--
THEN, FOR A LITTLE WHILE, AT LEAST...
...I REALLY DO BELIEVE.

...SHOW YOURSELF!
STOP HIDING FROM ME!
ALL THE TIME-- IN THE SHADOWS! BUT I KNOW YOU'RE THERE!
I CAN FEEL YOUR EYES ON ME!
WHAT DO YOU WANT? HAVEN'T YOU HURT ME ENOUGH?
YOU KILLED ME! YOU BURIED ME! WASN'T THAT ENOUGH?
WHY WON'T YOU LEAVE ME ALONE?!
THERE YOU ARE!
THERE YOU ARE!
BUT YOU'RE STILL HIDING, YOU COWARD!
YOU MISERABLE COWARD!

YOU THINK YOU CAN FOOL ME INTO BELIEVING YOU'RE DEAD? I KNOW YOU'RE NOT DEAD! I KNOW YOU'RE OUT THERE SOMEWHERE! BEHIND MY BACK-- OVER MY SHOULDER!
YOU'RE OUT THERE-- AND I'M GOING TO FIND YOU!

DO YOU HEAR ME? I'M GOING TO FIND YOU! YOU'RE NOT GOING TO DO IT TO ME AGAIN!
OH, GOD, HOW I HATE YOU!
HERE LIES KRAVEN THE HUNTER

I HATE YOU!
I HATE YOU!

...I...

LIES
DIED

THE DREAMS... EVERY NIGHT FOR WEEKS NOW. AND, WORSE-- AFTER THE DREAMS... WHEN I FEEL HIM ALL AROUND ME. ALL OVER ME-- LIKE A SECOND SKIN.
(HE'S HERE.)
NAGEL
I KEEP TELLING MYSELF IT'S NOT POSSIBLE. HE'S DEAD.
BUT-- WHAT IF HE'S NOT? I'VE BEEN TRICKED BEFORE. WHAT IF THIS WAS ALL PART OF SOME PLAN?

HIS CONFESSION, THE PHOTOS... ALL OF IT A...

(HE'S--)

...LIE.

(--HERE!!)
KRAVEN!

YOU'RE NOT REAL!
I'M STILL SLEEPING! STILL DREAMING!
YOU'RE NOT REAL!

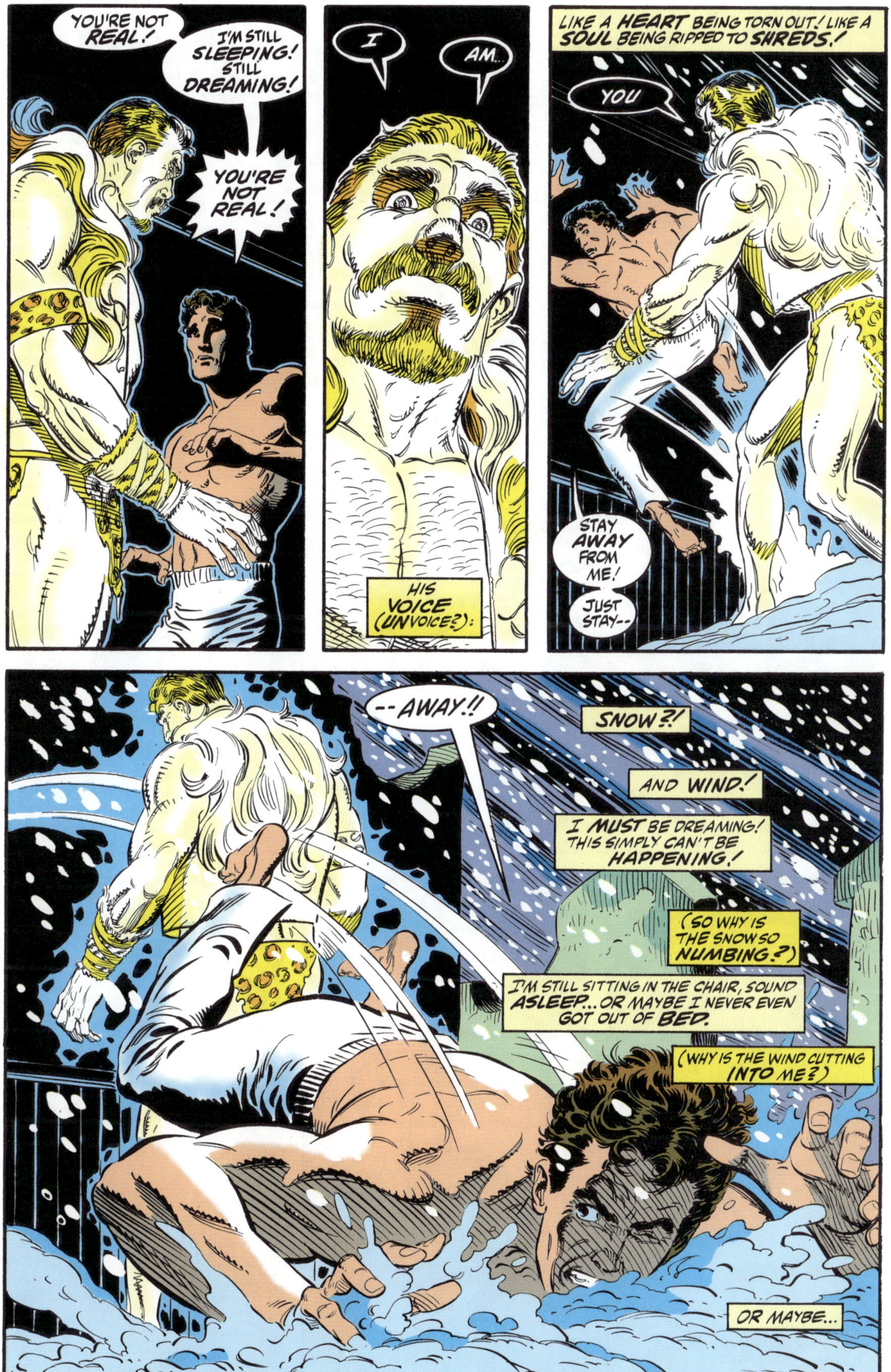

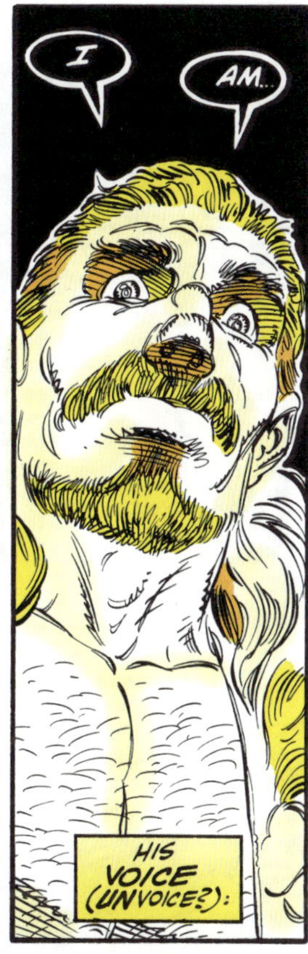
I
AM...
HIS VOICE (UNVOICE?):

LIKE A HEART BEING TORN OUT! LIKE A SOUL BEING RIPPED TO SHREDS!
YOU
STAY AWAY FROM ME!
JUST STAY--

--AWAY!!
SNOW?!
AND WIND!
I MUST BE DREAMING! THIS SIMPLY CAN'T BE HAPPENING!
(SO WHY IS THE SNOW SO NUMBING?)
I'M STILL SITTING IN THE CHAIR, SOUND ASLEEP... OR MAYBE I NEVER EVEN GOT OUT OF BED.
(WHY IS THE WIND CUTTING INTO ME?)
OR MAYBE...

DRUGS! THAT'S IT! LORD KNOWS HE'S DONE IT TO ME BEFORE-- WITH HIS HERBS AND ROOTS AND JUNGLE POTIONS!
MAYBE I'VE BEEN DRUGGED --AND THIS IS ALL SOME KIND OF HALLUCINATION!
lies
WHAT?
LIES!

MY... LIFE... WAS... LIES!!
LIES

THAT'S WHAT YOU ARE! THAT'S WHAT ALL OF THIS IS!
LIES!

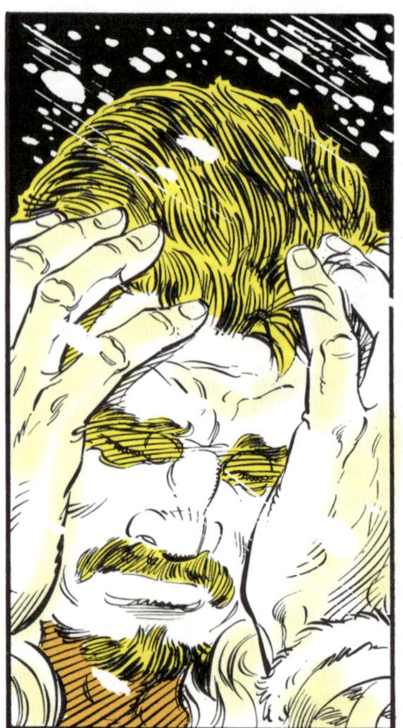

PLEASE...

KRAVEN--
--WHAT DO YOU WANT?

...BIGGER.

--ARE THE ONLY ONE WHO CAN GIVE IT TO HIM.

...PLEASE...

BE STILL, KRAVEN. THOUGH YOU HAVE THE APPEARANCE OF FORM-- YOU ARE ONLY A SHADOW--

--THE SHADOW OF A SHADOW.

I WILL SPEAK FOR YOU. I MUST SPEAK FOR YOU. THAT IS--WHY I AM.

THERE'S FEAR IN KRAVEN'S EYES; SUCH TERRIBLE FEAR. YET ALL I CAN SENSE FROM THAT... FORMLESS FORM IS A PEACE. A CALM. A...

... LOVE?
WHO ARE YOU?
WHO I AM DOESN'T MATTER. WHAT MATTERS IS YOU, PETER.
YOU... KRAVEN--

--AND THE BONDS YOU FORGED WHILE THE HUNTER LIVED.
I DON'T BELIEVE THIS... I DON'T BELIEVE ANY OF THIS.
(AND YET)
MAYBE IT'S A DREAM. MAYBE A FEVER. MAYBE I REALLY HAVE LOST MY MIND.
(AND YET)

AND YET THIS APPARITION SOMEHOW SEEMS MORE REAL TO ME-- THAN REALITY ITSELF.
TRUST ME, PETER, TRUST WHAT YOU FEEL IN THE DEEPEST PART OF YOU.
REAL--IN A WAY I'VE NEVER KNOWN.
THERE IS A CHOICE YOU MUST MAKE.
A CHOICE? WHAT DO YOU MEAN?

YOU ALONE, PETER--
--CAN SAVE THE HUNTER'S SOUL.

SAVE HIM? WHAT ARE YOU TALKING ABOUT?
SAVE A DEAD MAN?
NOT ALIVE--
I TRUST HIM. (HOW?) HER. (HOW?). NO... BEYOND "HIM" OR "HER"...
--BUT NO... NOT DEAD, EITHER.
LOOK, PETER--
...YET SOMEHOW CONTAINING (TRANSCENDING!) BOTH.
HOW CAN I TRUST A NIGHTMARE?
LOOK!
THE SKY!
THE SKY!
EXPLODING! A WHIRLPOOL OF LIGHT: SPINNING, SPINNING, SPINNING. THEN, THE LIGHT BECOMES FORM... AND THE FORM BECOMES...
...PEOPLE?!
SPIRITS. SHADOWS.
SUICIDES.
CAN YOU HEAR THEM, PETER? THEIR TORMENT, THEIR ANGUISH?
I HEAR. (BUT I DON'T WANT TO!) IT'S LIKE ALL THE PAIN I'VE EVER KNOWN IN MY LIFE... MAGNIFIED A THOUSAND TIMES! (I DON'T WANT TO!)
YOU MUST.

LISTEN TO THE ECHOES OF WASTED LIVES. LISTEN TO THE AGONY OF THE ONES TRAPPED--BETWEEN. TRAPPED--
-- JUST AS KRAVEN IS TRAPPED.
EACH SPIRIT HAS A PATH--AND FROM CRADLE TO GRAVE WE WALK IT: FALLING... STRUGGLING BACK TO OUR FEET... LEARNING FROM OUR STRUGGLES... AND MOVING ON.
BUT THE ONES WHO TURN AWAY FROM THE PATH...
...THE ONES WHO, WITH THEIR OWN HANDS, LET GO THE MOST PRECIOUS GIFT A SPIRIT CAN EVER RECEIVE--
--FIND THEMSELVES LOCKED TIGHT--
--IN A COFFIN OF THEIR OWN MAKING.
--ANY MORE THAN THEY CAN MOVE BACK.
THEY'VE LEFT THEIR LIFE'S WORK UNFINISHED, PETER... TURNED AWAY FROM THE PATH BEFORE IT'S REACHED ITS END... AND SO CANNOT MOVE ON--
BUT THERE IS HOPE FOR THESE LOST AND TORMENTED SOULS.
EACH SPIRIT HAS A LINK--ONE AMONG THE LIVING TO WHOM IT IS CONNECTED IN A... UNIQUE WAY. CALL IT DESTINY, KARMA... CALL IT WHAT YOU WILL--
--BUT THAT LINK... AMONG ALL WHO WALK THIS WORLD... IS THE ONLY ONE WHO CAN SAVE THE TRAPPED SPIRIT--
--FREE IT FROM BONDAGE.

AND FOR KRAVEN, PETER--
--YOU ARE THE LINK.
DREAMS.

YOU FORMED THE CENTER OF THE HUNTER'S UNIVERSE. THE CREATURE HE CALLED THE SPIDER WAS ALL THAT KRAVEN LIVED FOR... DIED FOR.
MADNESS.

NO MATTER THAT IT WAS ALL A CREATION OF KRAVEN'S TWISTED MIND...NO MATTER THAT THE HONOR HE THOUGHT HE'D FIND IN DEATH WAS AS MUCH A LIE AS THE SPIDER ITSELF--
FEVER.

YOUR LINK IS REAL. FAR DEEPER... AND OF LONGER DURATION... THAN YOU COULD EVER IMAGINE.
LIES.

SO I ASK YOU, PETER, TO FACE A TRIAL UNLIKE ANY YOU'VE EVER FACED BEFORE.
(BUT WHAT--)
I ASK YOU TO STRUGGLE AND SUFFER, NOT FOR YOURSELF-- BUT FOR THE REDEMPTION OF A TORTURED SOUL.
(BUT WHAT IF--)
WILL YOU DO IT, PETER?
(BUT WHAT IF IT'S TRUE?)

NO!
YOU THINK I'D DO ANYTHING TO SAVE HIM?! HELP HIM?!
OH, GOD, IF THIS WAS REALLY HAPPENING... I'D WANT TO KNOW THAT-- FOR ALL ETERNITY-- THAT ANIMAL WOULD SUFFER FOR WHAT HE DID TO ME!
DO YOU HEAR ME, KRAVEN--

--FOR ALL ETERNITY!!
NO, KRAVEN: NOT A SOUND. NOT A MOVEMENT.

HE'S MADE HIS DECISION --
AND I MEANT IT. I MEANT EVERY WORD.
--AND WE MUST ABIDE BY IT.
--eter...?
SO WHY DO I FEEL SO...
Peter...?

SWEETIE-- WHAT ARE YOU DOING?
...GUILTY?
HUH? WHAT?
I HEARD YOU GET UP OUT OF BED, HON. IS EVERYTHING ALL RIGHT?

WHY DON'T I MAKE US SOME TEA AND--
GOD, YOUR HANDS ARE LIKE ICE.

I SAW HIS GHOST.
WHAT?
I SAW KRAVEN'S GHOST.

SO I TELL HER. WHAT ELSE CAN I DO? SHE'S MY WIFE. MY PARTNER. MY BEST FRIEND.
WHAT ELSE CAN I DO?
...YOU THINK I'VE REALLY LOST IT THIS TIME, DON'T YOU?
YOU THINK I'M OUT OF MY MIND--
NO.
C'MON, M.J.--DON'T GIVE ME--

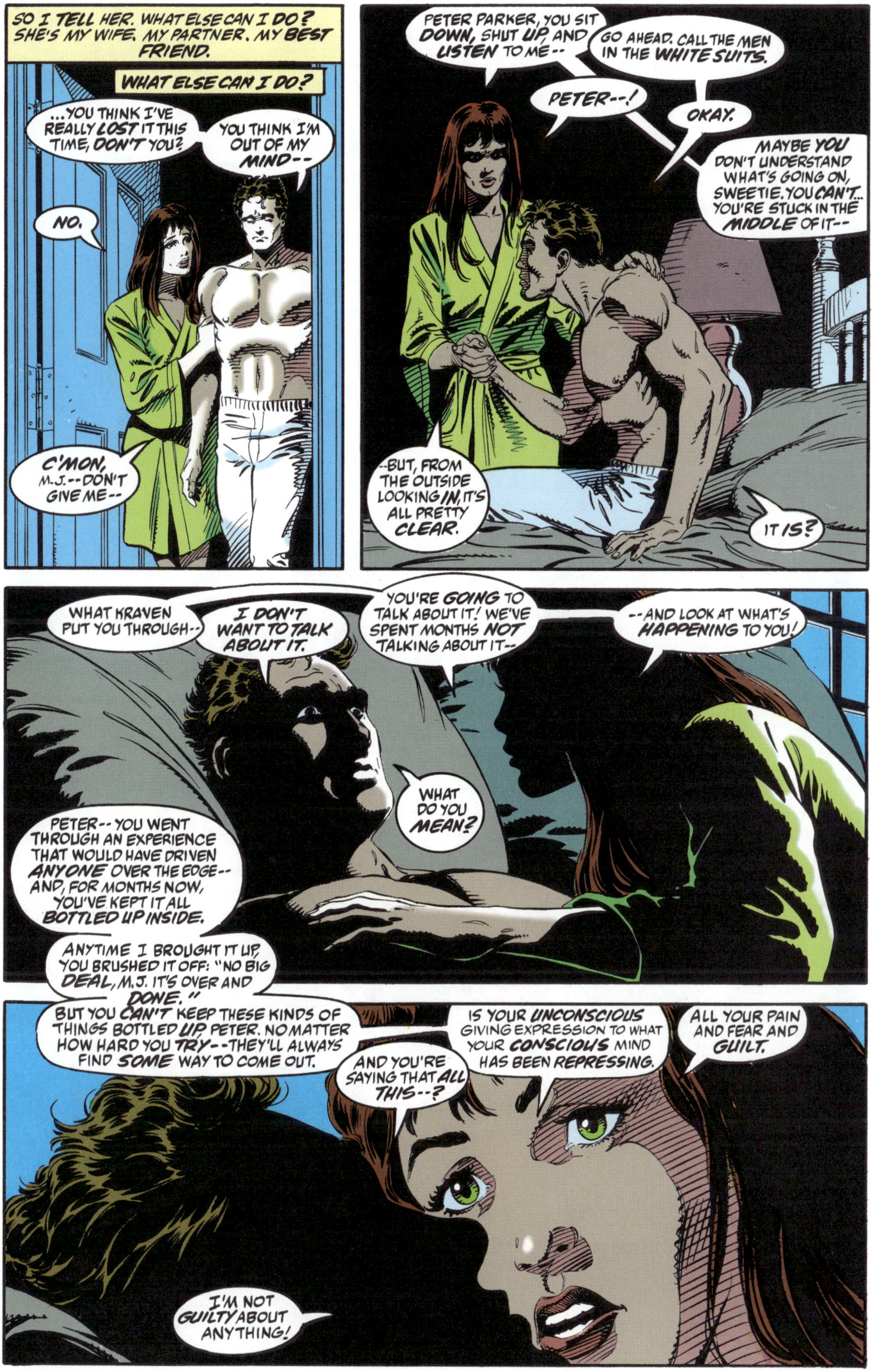

PETER PARKER, YOU SIT DOWN, SHUT UP, AND LISTEN TO ME--
GO AHEAD. CALL THE MEN IN THE WHITE SUITS.
PETER--!
OKAY.
MAYBE YOU DON'T UNDERSTAND WHAT'S GOING ON, SWEETIE. YOU CAN'T... YOU'RE STUCK IN THE MIDDLE OF IT--
--BUT, FROM THE OUTSIDE LOOKING IN, IT'S ALL PRETTY CLEAR.
IT IS?

WHAT KRAVEN PUT YOU THROUGH--
I DON'T WANT TO TALK ABOUT IT.
YOU'RE GOING TO TALK ABOUT IT! WE'VE SPENT MONTHS NOT TALKING ABOUT IT--
--AND LOOK AT WHAT'S HAPPENING TO YOU!
WHAT DO YOU MEAN?
PETER--YOU WENT THROUGH AN EXPERIENCE THAT WOULD HAVE DRIVEN ANYONE OVER THE EDGE--AND, FOR MONTHS NOW, YOU'VE KEPT IT ALL BOTTLED UP INSIDE.
ANYTIME I BROUGHT IT UP, YOU BRUSHED IT OFF: "NO BIG DEAL, M.J. IT'S OVER AND DONE."

BUT YOU CAN'T KEEP THESE KINDS OF THINGS BOTTLED UP, PETER. NO MATTER HOW HARD YOU TRY--THEY'LL ALWAYS FIND SOME WAY TO COME OUT.
AND YOU'RE SAYING THAT ALL THIS--?
IS YOUR UNCONSCIOUS GIVING EXPRESSION TO WHAT YOUR CONSCIOUS MIND HAS BEEN REPRESSING.
ALL YOUR PAIN AND FEAR AND GUILT.
I'M NOT GUILTY ABOUT ANYTHING!

PETER PARKER-- YOU WERE BORN GUILTY!
KRAVEN MAY HAVE BEEN YOUR ENEMY--BUT, MY GOD, THE MAN KILLED HIMSELF! AND SOMEWHERE INSIDE YOU IS A VOICE SAYING: "I COULD HAVE STOPPED HIM. I COULD HAVE SAVED HIM."
NO, NEVER.
YES. ALWAYS.
THAT'S WHAT MAKES YOU YOU. THAT'S ONE OF THE REASONS WHY I LOVE YOU.
THERE'S A PART OF YOU THAT WANTS TO SAVE THE WHOLE WORLD. THAT WANTS TO TAKE ALL THE SUFFERING OUT THERE AND MAGICALLY... WEB IT AWAY.
BUT IT DOESN'T WORK THAT WAY, PETER. AND IF YOU DON'T GET SOME HELP WITH THIS--IT'S GOING TO KEEP EATING AWAY AT YOU. AT US.

SO WHAT DO YOU SUGGEST I DO? WALK INTO SOME THERAPIST'S OFFICE AND SAY, "HI, DOC, I'M SPIDER-MAN. KRAVEN THE HUNTER KILLED ME, THEN KILLED HIMSELF... AND I FEEL JUST AWFUL ABOUT IT"?
NOT EXACTLY, BUT--
NO, HONEY. THERE'S ONLY ONE WAY TO SEE THIS THROUGH--
WHAT ARE YOU TALKING ABOUT? WHERE DO YOU THINK YOU'RE GOING?
PETER--!

PETER--!
HEY-- DON'T WORRY. IT'S WHAT MAKES ME ME, REMEMBER? IT'S ONE OF THE REASONS WHY YOU LOVE ME.
I NEVER SAID THAT.
OH, YES, YOU DID. AND I LOVE YOU, DARLIN'--

--MORE THAN MY LIFE.

HERE LIES
SERGEI
KRAVINOFF
KRAVEN THE HUNTER
HE DIED WITH
HONOR

WHAT AM I DOING HERE? WHAT AM I EXPECTING TO FIND?

MAYBE NOTHING. MAYBE JUST COMING BACK TO WHERE IT HAPPENED (WHERE HE BURIED ME!) WILL BE ENOUGH TO LAY IT TO REST ONCE AND FOR ALL.
(HE BURIED ME!)

OR MAYBE--
YOU CAME.

REAL? IMAGINED? DOES IT REALLY MATTER?
WHAT IS IT? WHAT DO YOU WANT ME TO DO?
IT'S NOT WHAT I WANT YOU TO DO--
--BUT WHAT YOU MUST CHOOSE TO DO--
TELL ME!

WAIT--

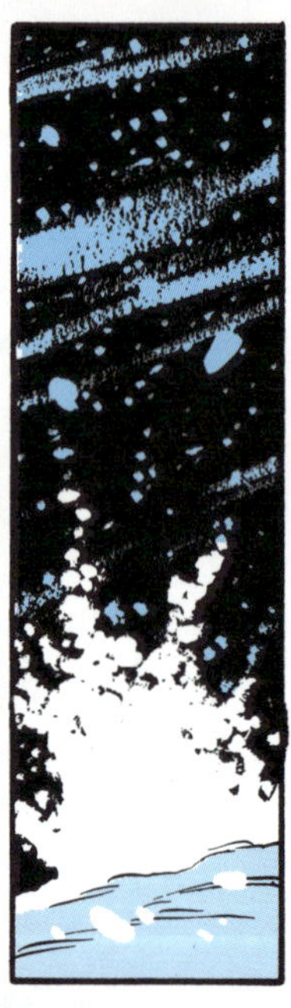

NOW WE CAN BEGIN.

BEGIN WHAT?
YOU SAID BEFORE THAT I'D HAVE TO FACE SOME TRIAL--
UNLIKE ANY YOU'VE EVER FACED BEFORE.
WHAT IS IT?!

REAL?

IMAGINED?

DOES IT REALLY MATTER?

THE SPIRIT STANDS BESIDE ME: LESS SUBSTANTIAL THAN THE WIND. THE BODY RISES UP IN FRONT OF ME: DEEP AND DARK AS THE EARTH.
I DON'T KNOW IF I'M SANE-- OR IF I'VE FINALLY STAGGERED OVER THE EDGE. I JUST KNOW THAT I'M AFRAID.
I CAN'T STAY HERE!
AND I WON'T!
YOU CAN'T EXPECT ME TO FIGHT--THAT!

THE CHOICE IS YOURS.
SUCH PEACE. JUST TO HEAR HIM (NOT HIM. NOT HER. SOMETHING... BIGGER.) SPEAK...
...FILLS ME WITH PEACE. DRAINS ME OF ANGER. AND UP THERE ABOVE ME:

THEY'RE SINGING TO ME... THE SPIRITS OF THE SUICIDES.
A SONG OF SUFFERING DEEPER THAN ANY I'VE EVER KNOWN. AND A SONG OF HOPE--NOT JUST FOR KRAVEN... NOT JUST FOR THEMSELVES...

...BUT FOR...
...ME?
SOMETHING IN THEIR STRANGE AND AWFUL SONG, SOMETHING IN THAT SHROUDED BEING'S VOICELESS VOICE, REACHES A PLACE IN ME BEYOND WORDS, BEYOND THOUGHT. AND I KNOW:

I'LL DO IT.
I'M NOT SURE WHY...

...BUT I'LL DO IT.
(DON'T! DON'T!)

MISSED HIM!
GOOD! DON'T TOUCH HIM! RUN!)
OH, GOD... LOOK AT HIM! FILTH AND ROT AND...
(RUN!)
...THE STENCH! EVEN THROUGH MY MASK, IT'S...

(RUN!)
...HORRIBLE!
RUN, YOU IDIOT! RUN FAR AWAY!
GET OUT OF HERE BEFORE HE DOES IT TO YOU AGAIN! BEFORE HE DRAGS YOU BACK...

DOWN
INTO
THE
DARK.

...NUHHHHHH...

NO!
I KNOW WHAT YOU'RE THINKING-- AND IT'S NOT TRUE!!
IT'S NOT MY FAULT YOU'RE DEAD!

IT'S NOT!!

PEOPLE HURT... PEOPLE DIE... EVERY DAY! THAT'S THE WAY IT IS! I CAN'T BRING ANY-ONE BACK!

I CAN'T SAVE ANYONE'S SOUL!

I'M JUST ONE MAN!
MOVE IT, PARKER... MOVE IT! YOU DON'T OWE ANYONE ANYTHING! YOU DON'T HAVE TO DO THIS!
SO MOVE-- AND PUT AS MUCH DISTANCE BETWEEN YOU AND THAT HIDEOUS THING AS YOU POSSIBLY...

...CAN...?!
STOP IT! WHY WON'T YOU STOP IT?!?
I DIDN'T KNOW YOU WERE GOING TO KILL YOURSELF! IF I HAD KNOWN--

(THE SONG: NOT JUST SUFFERING--BUT HOPE.)

--DON'T YOU THINK I WOULD HAVE DONE SOMETHING?! I SWEAR TO YOU--

--I WOULDN'T HAVE--
--LET YOU--
--DIE!

"LIKE YOU LET YOUR UNCLE BEN DIE?"
HE DOESN'T HAVE TO SPEAK THE WORDS FOR ME TO HEAR THEM. I CAN FEEL THEM--IN MY HEART.
"REMEMBER, ALL THOSE YEARS AGO, WHEN YOU WERE TOO WRAPPED UP IN YOURSELF TO BE BOTHERED WITH OTHER PEOPLE'S PROBLEMS?
"WHEN YOU LET THAT TWO-BIT HOOD GET BY YOU? THE SAME MAN WHO BROKE INTO YOUR HOUSE THAT NIGHT...

(FOR KRAVEN.)

"...AND KILLED YOUR UNCLE BEN?"

BUT IT'S NOT THE SAME THING!
ALL THESE YEARS--I'VE DONE MY BEST TO MAKE UP FOR THAT! I'VE WORN THIS SUIT--GONE OUT THERE AND PUT MY LIFE ON THE LINE AGAIN AND AGAIN!

BUT NO MATTER HOW HARD I TRY--

(FOR ME?)

--PEOPLE--

--DIE!
HERE LIES
SPIDER-MAN
SLAIN BY THE
HUNTER
THE GROUND. THE GRAVE. THE DARK. THE DEAD.

CAPTAIN STACY. GWEN. NED.
KRAVEN.

-- AND I DON'T WANT TO DIE!

BUT I HAVE TO DIE, DON'T I?

IT'S MY FAULT.

I COULD HAVE SAVED THEM-- AND I DIDN'T.
SO I HAVE TO DIE...

...TOO?

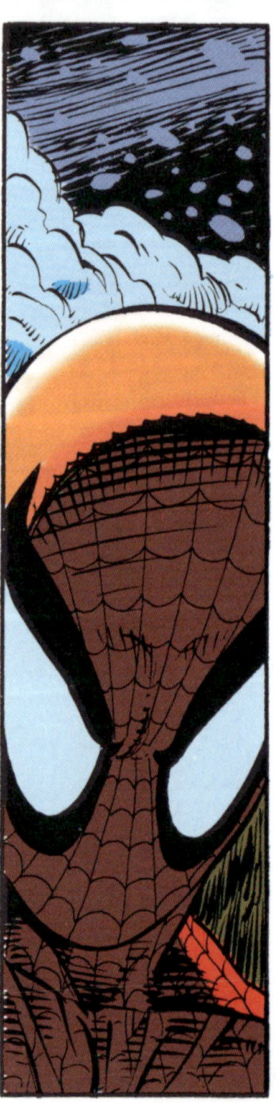

DIE?

TURN MY BACK ON THE MOST PRECIOUS GIFT THERE IS?

WHY? BECAUSE LIFE'S A STRUGGLE? BECAUSE WE MAKE MISTAKES? BECAUSE WE HURT?
NO! IF UNCLE BEN'S DEATH TAUGHT ME ANYTHING--IT'S THAT WE HAVE TO LEARN FROM OUR SUFFERING--NOT RUN AWAY FROM IT!

I'M NOT TAKING THE COWARD'S WAY OUT!
I'M
NOT!

OF COURSE LIFE IS HARD SOMETIMES--HARD AND FULL OF PAIN--
--BUT THERE'S JOY, TOO--JOY AND LOVE--IF YOU'VE GOT THE COURAGE TO LOOK FOR THEM!

BEN PARKER KNEW THAT! HE LIVED THAT!
AND MARY JANE--EVERY DAY, SHE SHOWS ME MORE LOVE THAN I EVER DREAMED THERE COULD BE IN THE WORLD!
BUT KRAVEN--HE NEVER LOOKED FOR THE LOVE, DID HE?
ALL HE COULD DO WAS STARE INTO THE DARKNESS--AND CURSE HIS FATE!

I DON'T KNOW WHAT AWFUL THINGS TWISTED HIM SO...OR WHAT FINALLY BROKE HIS SPIRIT--
--BUT I WON'T BE BROKEN LIKE THAT!
I CHOOSE LIFE!

I CHOOSE LIFE!

I'M FREE.

AND SO IS HE.

MAYBE WE CAN NEVER KNOW FOR SURE IF THERE'S A LARGER MEANING TO OUR LIVES... A PURPOSE AND A PLAN--BUT WE CAN MAKE A CHOICE...
...TO LISTEN HARD FOR A SONG OF HOPE...

...A SONG OF BELIEF IN SOMETHING BIGGER...

REST IN PEACE, KRAVEN.
...THAT EVERY HEART CAN TOUCH...

...WHEN IT OPENS IN LOVE.
REST IN PEACE.

...DON'T YOU SEE, PETER? YOUR MIND WAS SICK--AND IT CREATED THIS WHOLE THING WITH KRAVEN'S GHOST AND THAT WHOLE GRAVEYARD BATTLE--
M.J.--
--AS A WAY TO HEAL ITSELF. TO WORK OUT ALL THE--
M.J.--

15
YOU DON'T WANT TO TALK ABOUT IT?
NO. WELL...YES. BUT IT'S NOT LIKE BEFORE--WHEN I WAS AFRAID TO TALK ABOUT IT. IT'S JUST THAT--

202
WELL, SOME THINGS TOUCH US IN A PLACE THAT WORDS CAN'T EVER REALLY REACH--
--AND WHAT I FELT THERE--AT THE END--TO TALK ABOUT IT TOO MUCH, OVER-ANALYZE IT--

YOU DON'T WANT TO CHEAPEN IT WITH WORDS?
NOK NOK

203

...UNCLE GEORGE... AUNT HANNAH-- THESE ARE MY FRIENDS, PETER AND MARY JANE PARKER--
PLEASURE TO MEET YOU.
THERE'S ENOUGH FOOD TO FEED AN ARMY. SIT. WE'LL GET YOU SOMETHING TO EAT.
YOU DON'T HAVE TO DO THAT. WE CAN HELP OUR--
JUST SIT--TALK TO ROGER. WE'LL TAKE CARE OF EVERYTHING.

SO--HOW ARE YOU, ROG?
...THEY'VE BEEN GREAT. WELL, ACTUALLY, THEY'VE BEEN DRIVING ME UP THE WALL--BUT THEY MEAN WELL--
DAYS ARE PRETTY GOOD. BUT THE NIGHTS--
IT TAKES TIME.
I KNOW. BUT ALL THINGS CONSIDERED--I'M DOING A LOT BETTER THAN I EXPECTED TO.

S'FUNNY. I'M NOT VERY RELIGIOUS. AND MOM WAS PRACTICALLY AN ATHEIST. "ANY GOD WHO COULD LET HITLER DO WHAT HE DID," SHE USED TO SAY, "IS NO GOD OF MINE."
BUT THE OLD RITUALS--LIKE THIS SITTING SHIVA... MOURNING FOR SEVEN DAYS--THEY REALLY HELP. PEOPLE COME AND WE TALK ABOUT MOM... REMEMBER THE GOOD THINGS--AND EVEN THE NOT-SO-GOOD THINGS--
--AND IT'S LIKE I CAN FEEL HER HERE WITH ME. ALMOST LIKE HER... SPIRIT'S IN THE ROOM--JUST HOVERING THERE.
SPIRIT--?

I KNOW IT SOUNDS CRAZY-- BUT IT'S LIKE SHE'S BEEN TELLING ME SHE'S ALL RIGHT... THAT SHE'S IN A GOOD PLACE-- AND SHE'S BEING WELL TAKEN CARE OF--
CRAZY, RIGHT?
NO, ROGER.
NO.
I DON'T THINK IT'S CRAZY AT ALL.
HERE LIES
SERGEI KRAVINOFF
KRAVEN THE HUNTER
FREE AT LAST